POEMS THE U

This book has been selected to receive financial assistance from English PEN's 'PEN Translates' programme, supported by Arts Council England. English PEN exists to promote literature and our understanding of it, to uphold writers' freedoms around the world, to campaign against the persecution and imprisonment of writers for stating their views, and to promote the friendly co-operation of writers and the free exchange of ideas. www.englishpen.org

Poems the wind blew in

POEMS BY KARMELO C. IRIBARREN
TRANSLATED BY LAWRENCE SCHIMEL
ILLUSTRATED BY RIYA CHOWDHURY

THE EMMA PRESS

THE EMMA PRESS

First published in Spain as *Versos que el viento arrastra* by
Ediciones El Jinete Azul in 2010.
© *Versos que el viento arrastra* by Karmelo C. Iribarren 2010.

First published in the UK in 2019 by the Emma Press Ltd.
English translation © Lawrence Schimel 2019.
Illustrations © Riya Chowdhury 2019.

This book has been selected to receive financial assistance
from English PEN's 'PEN Translates' programme.

All rights reserved.

The right of Karmelo C. Iribarren, Lawrence Schimel and
Riya Chowdhury to be identified as the creators of this
work has been asserted in accordance with the Copyright,
Designs and Patents Act 1988.

ISBN 978-1-912915-31-6

A CIP catalogue record of this book is available
from the British Library.

Printed and bound in the UK by Imprint Digital, Exeter.

The Emma Press
theemmapress.com
hello@theemmapress.com
Jewellery Quarter,
Birmingham, UK

CONTENTS

Books 1

An ordinary day 2

Summer afternoon 5

Plastic bag 6

What the streetlight says 9

Things that happen in the sky 11

23rd floor 13

The still bicycles 14

This morning, in the park 16

Buddies 19

And they look so serious 20

Sadness 23

Small impressions 24

Short days, minuscule nights 27

Stations 29

Things of love 31

The rhythm of the wind *32*

Time 35

The smoke 37

The wind 39

When the storm comes 41

Detective birds 43

The distant rain 45

A special girl 47

Mysterious poems *48*

Night 51

The hotel 53

In some places 55

Dawning 56

BONUS BITS

Write your own poem 59

Interview with the translator 62

Learn some Spanish 66

WHO MADE THIS BOOK?

About the poet 69

About the translator 70

About the illustrator 71

About The Emma Press 72

About English PEN 73

Also from The Emma Press 74

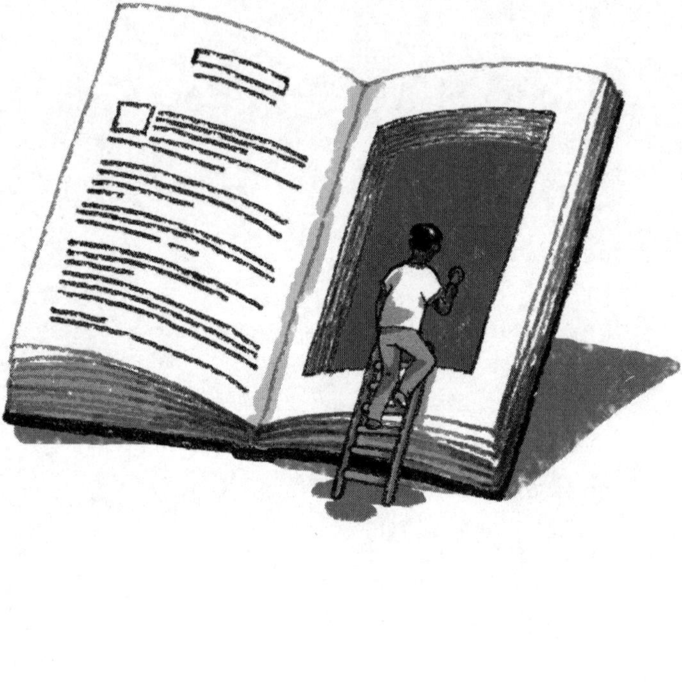

BOOKS

Books
are not there to be stared at:
they're meant to be touched,
opened
and read,
which is how you get inside them.

Try it and you'll see.

They remind you
of when you travelled
to a different city
and everything seemed new to you,
surprising,
and even a little bit
mysterious.

AN ORDINARY DAY

The wind is the fastest reader of newspapers in the world.

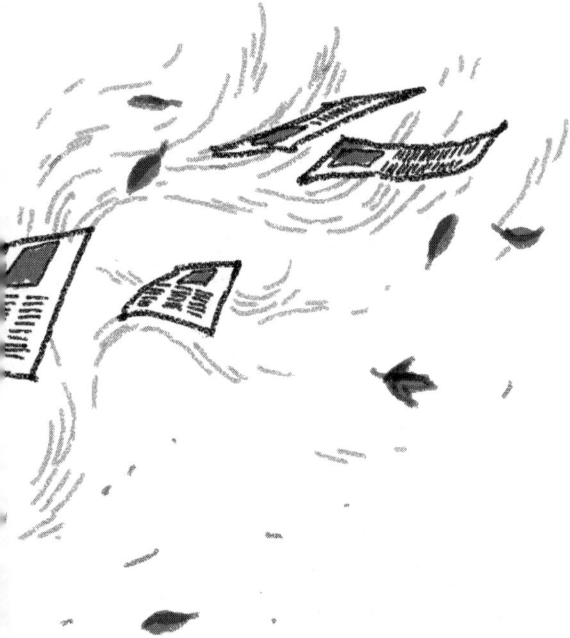

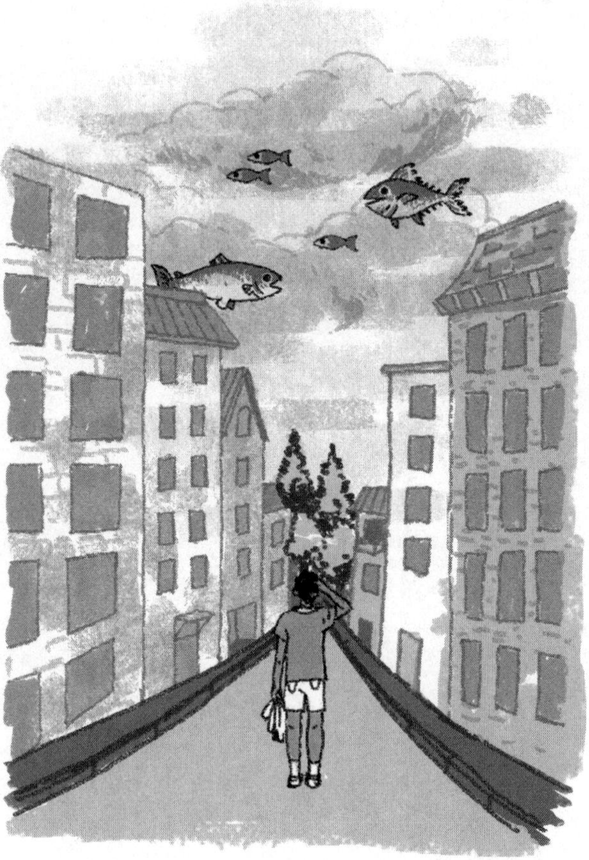

SUMMER AFTERNOON

From here,
squeezed
between the buildings,
the sky,

more than sky,
looks like a pool.
As if the day has been turned
upside down.

PLASTIC BAG

Look at it
there
in the middle of the street,
alone,
motionless,

afraid
that a street sweeper might appear,

dreaming
of a bit of wind
to make it feel
like a cloud.

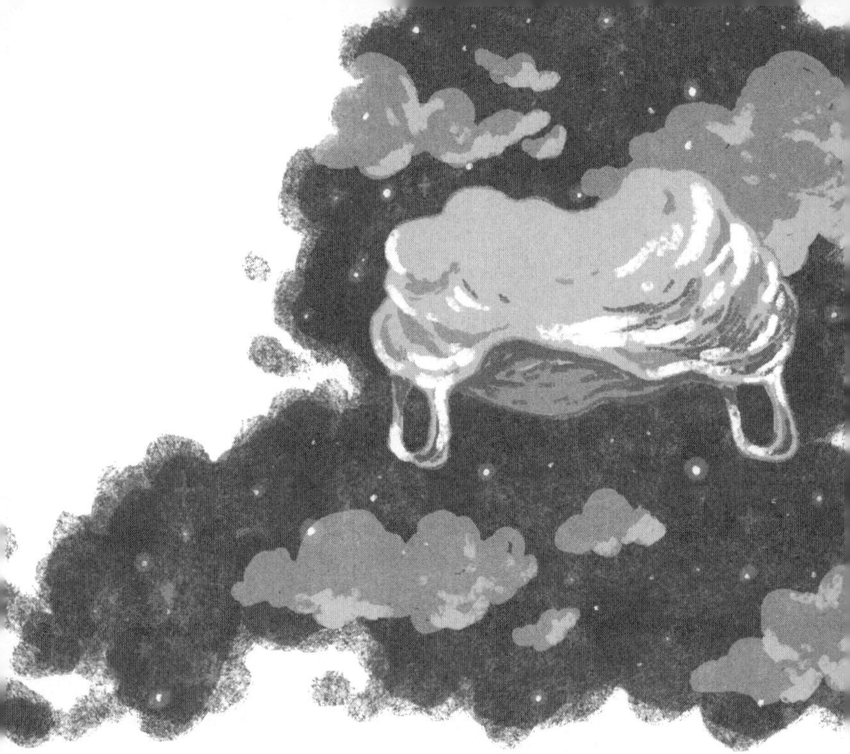

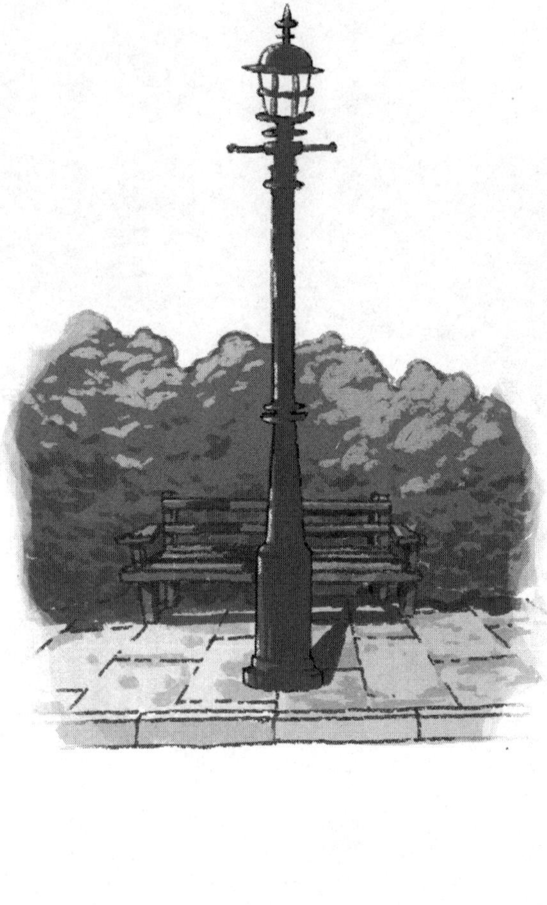

WHAT THE STREETLIGHT SAYS

What a
humiliating life:

by day
the dogs
and at night
the drunks.

Why
wasn't I born
a table lamp?

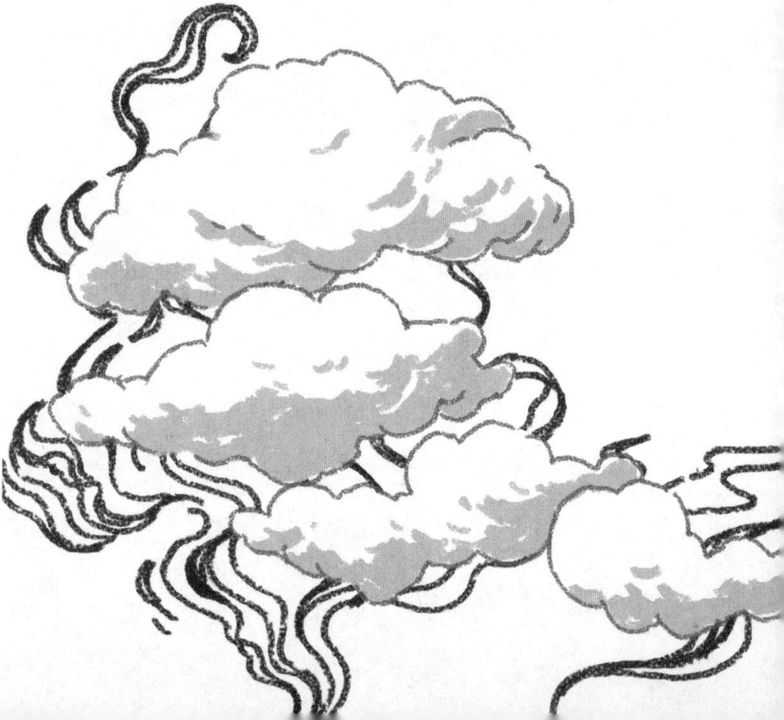

THINGS THAT HAPPEN IN THE SKY

Look,
up there,
those clouds
so white
so cheeky

putting themselves
right in front of the wind
so that it gives them a push

and behind them
the poor smoke from the chimney

unable to reach them

sweating soot.

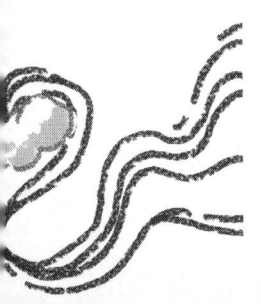

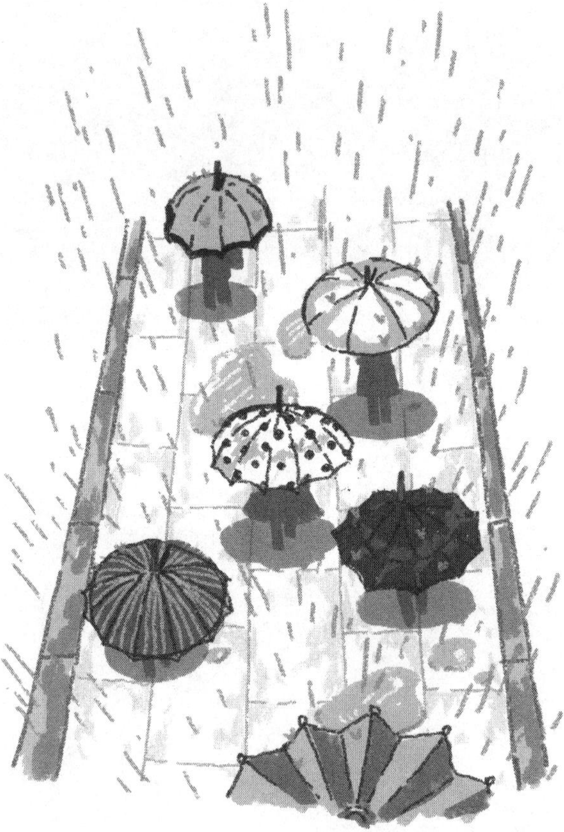

23RD FLOOR

From here,
up above,
the street
is spectacular,
magical,
full
of brightly-coloured
umbrellas.

It makes you want
to open one

and parachute
down.

THE STILL BICYCLES

Those bicycles
parked
on the street

in a row,
one beside the other,

look like vendors of kilometres
that no one is buying.

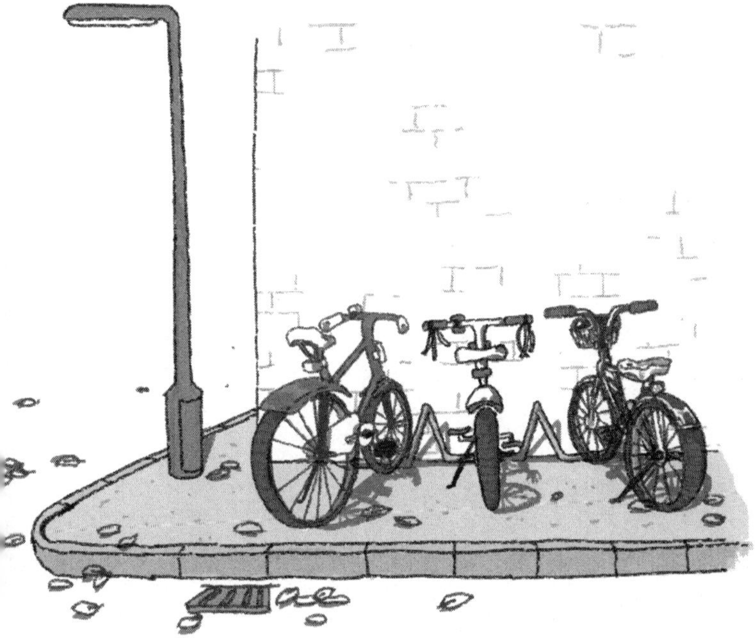

THIS MORNING, IN THE PARK

You really had to see it,

the grandfather
and the grandson,

both of them
wearing shorts
and a hat,

sitting
on a bench

in the shade

counting pigeons.

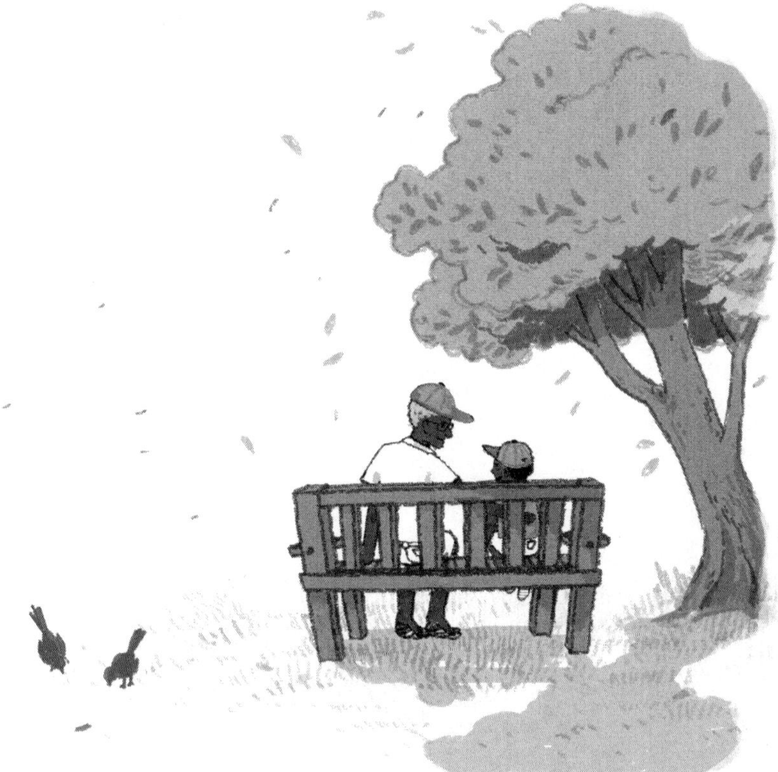

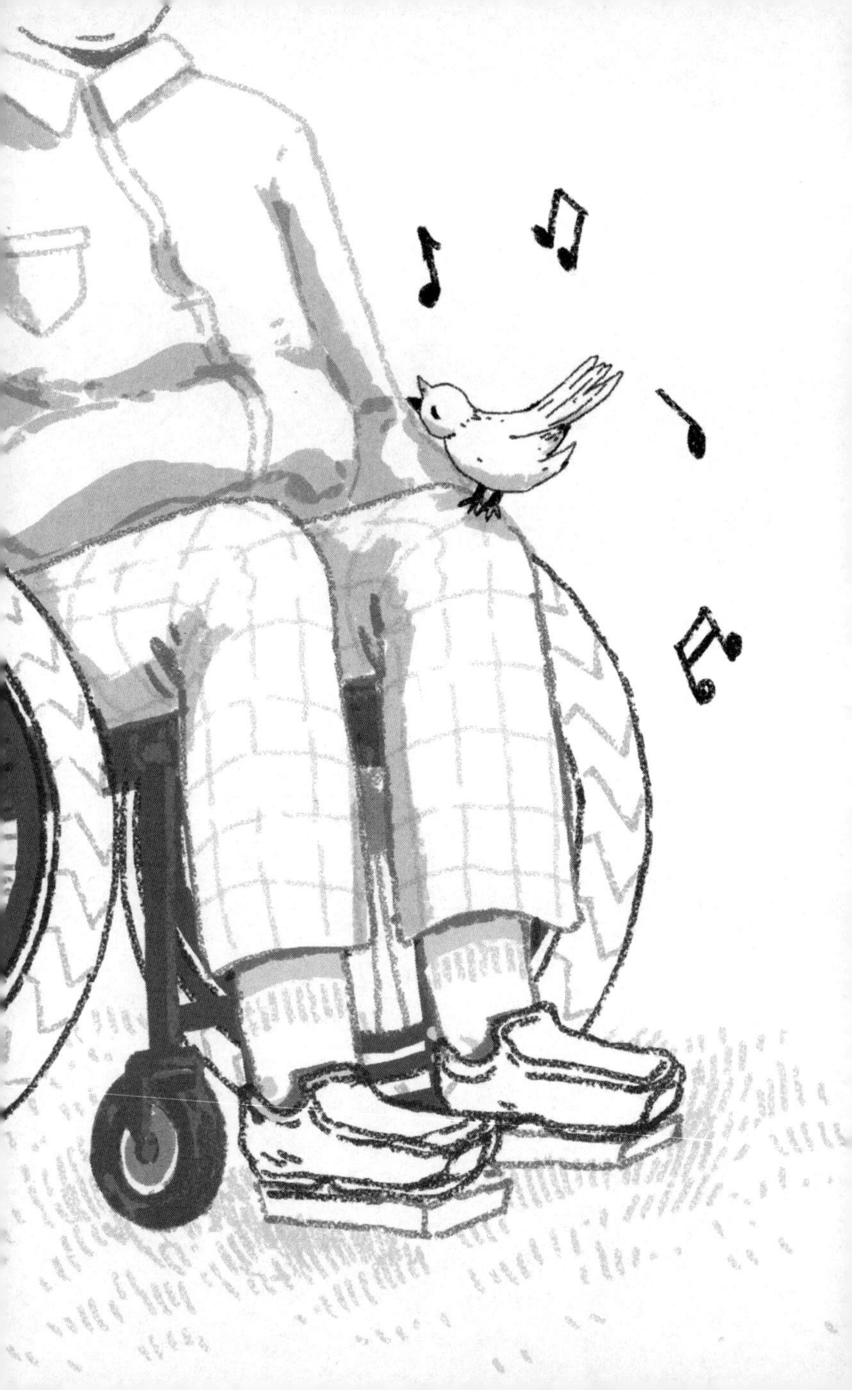

BUDDIES

The sparrow
and the paraplegic
live such different lives
that they always have things
to tell one another:

that's why
you can see them together
sometimes
in the park.

AND THEY LOOK SO SERIOUS

The statues
laugh
at the weather:

rain, heat,
winter, summer...

Bah!

Foolish things
of human
beings.

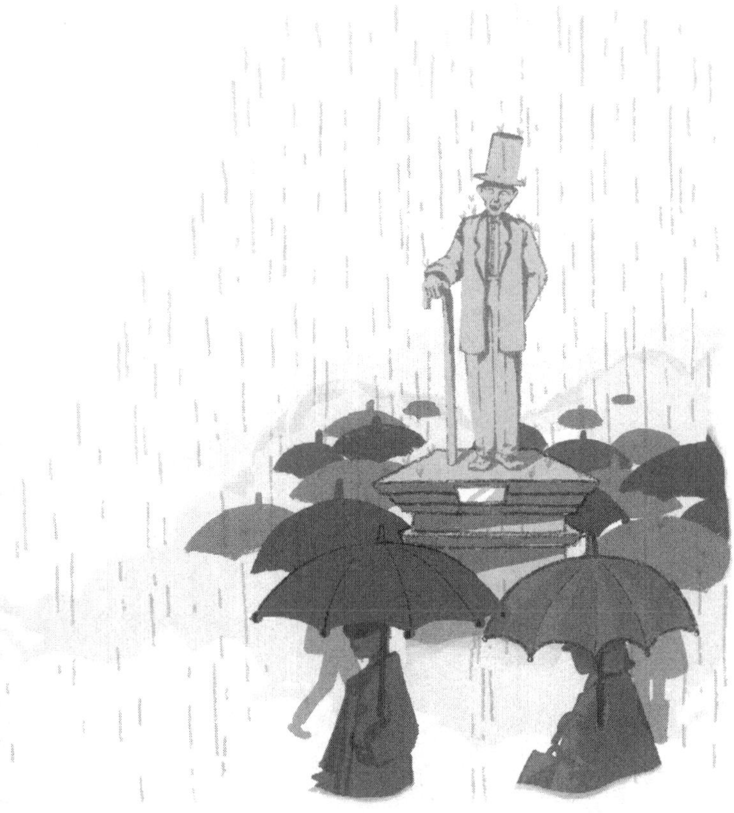

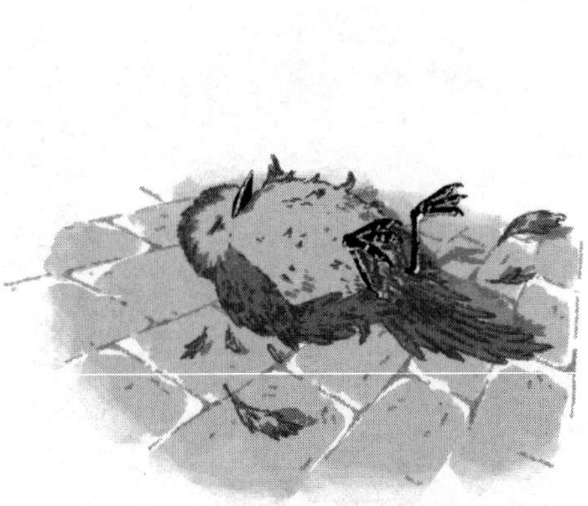

SADNESS

A sparrow
dead
on the pavement:

a trick sadness plays,
to tell us it exists,

without making us
feel very, very sad.

SMALL IMPRESSIONS

Hats
seem so serious
because they're full
of thoughts.

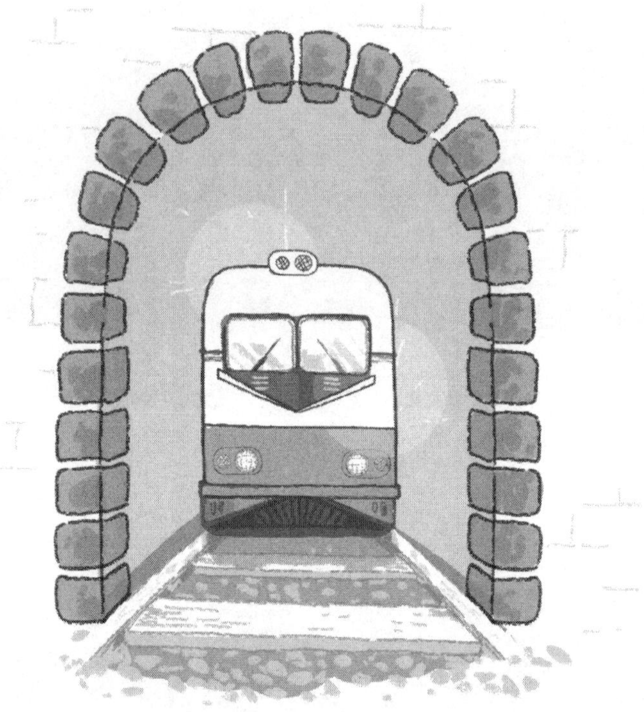

SHORT DAYS, MINUSCULE NIGHTS

How short the days seem
and how minuscule the nights
when you're sitting
on a train
that goes through lots of tunnels.

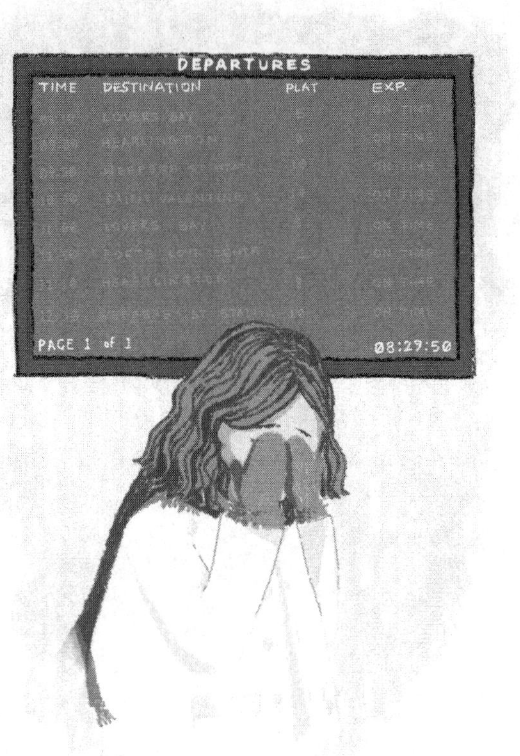
DEPARTURES
TIME
DESTINATION
PLAT
EXP.
PAGE 1 of 1
08:29:50

STATIONS

Stations
are there
for three very important things:

for trains to arrive,

for them to leave again,

and for lovers to cry.

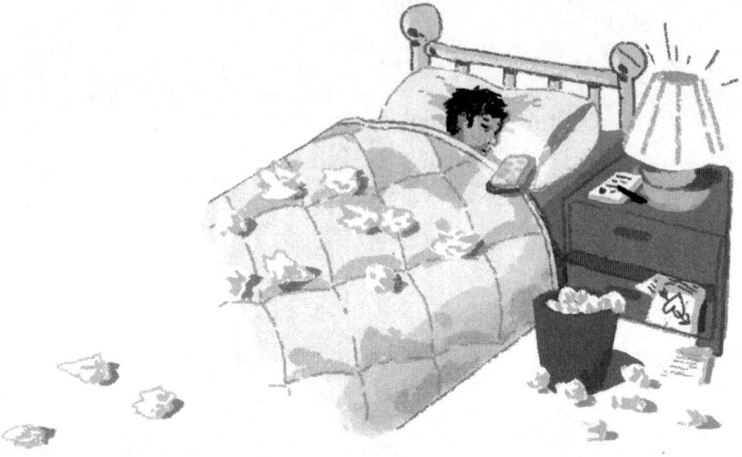

THINGS OF LOVE

The word *distance*
is very suggestive:

it makes life
seem broad,
it makes you dream.

Yes, I like how it sounds.

But sometimes
it comes between us
and then
I hate it –
I don't even want to see it

even if it comes after
the word *short*.

THE RHYTHM OF THE WIND

The trees
don't like
the wind
because
it makes them
sweep
the sky.

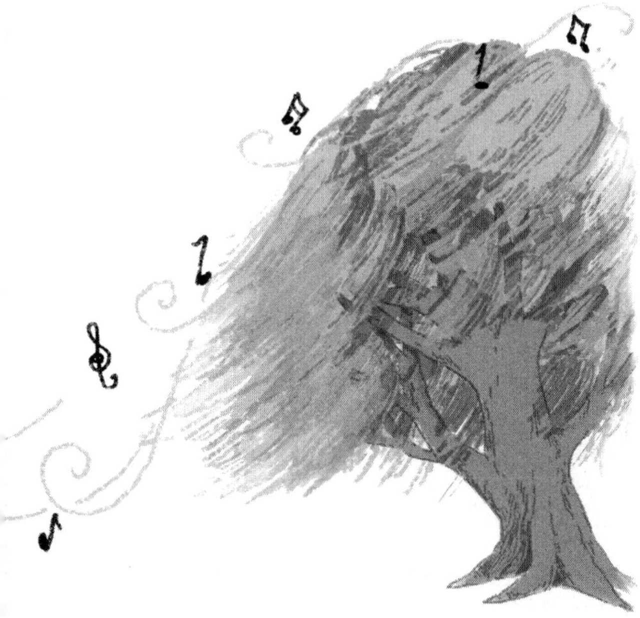

TIME

It's incredible,
time:

it doesn't stop
spinning,

doesn't go
anywhere,

doesn't sleep

and lives
in a watch.

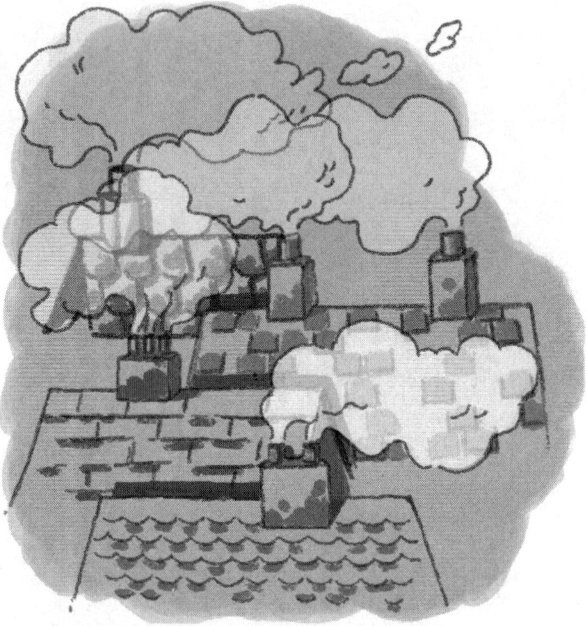

THE SMOKE

As if it feared
that it might be stopped

the smoke from the chimney
climbed quickly
towards the grey sky,

to camouflage itself.

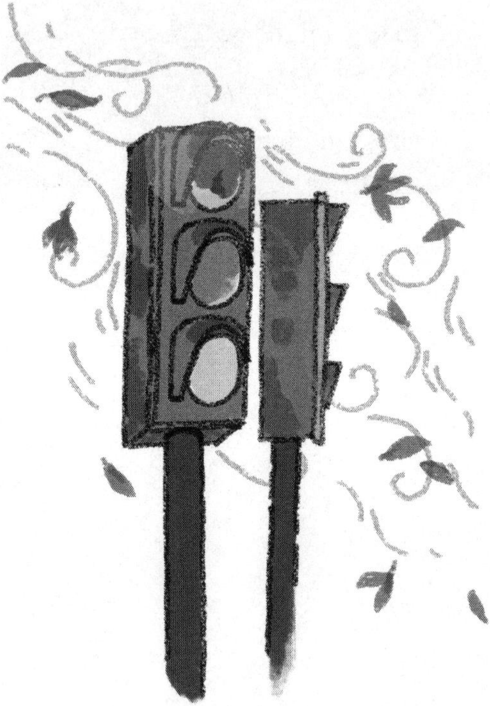

THE WIND

When the wind arrives
in the city
it always moves just like it's blind
and blunders into everything:

the trees,
the road signs,
the traffic lights,
the corners...

After all that, it looks
just pitiful,
dreadful.

That's why
a long time ago
it became invisible.

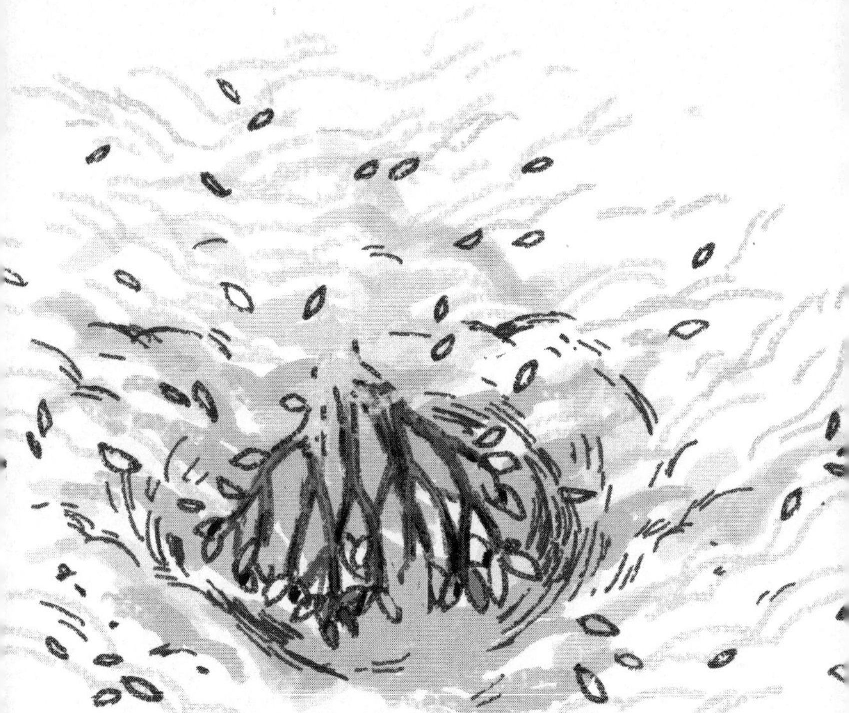

WHEN THE STORM COMES

The wind
has blown in,

the trees
are now
green brooms,

the clouds
hurry off quickly
so they're not swept away.

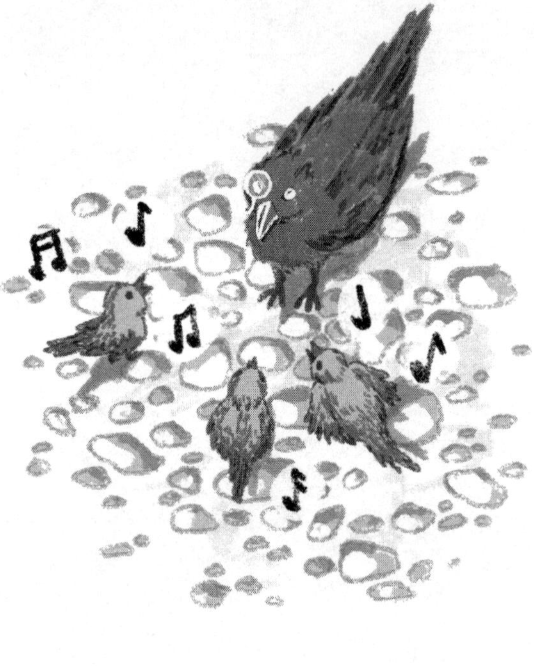

DETECTIVE BIRDS

Three swallows
on a telephone
wire,
motionless,
very serious,
very attentive.
Soon,
one takes flight,
then another,
then the third.
They don't need
to hear more –
it's enough.
They go to tell
the raven.
Who was right.
It was the canary.

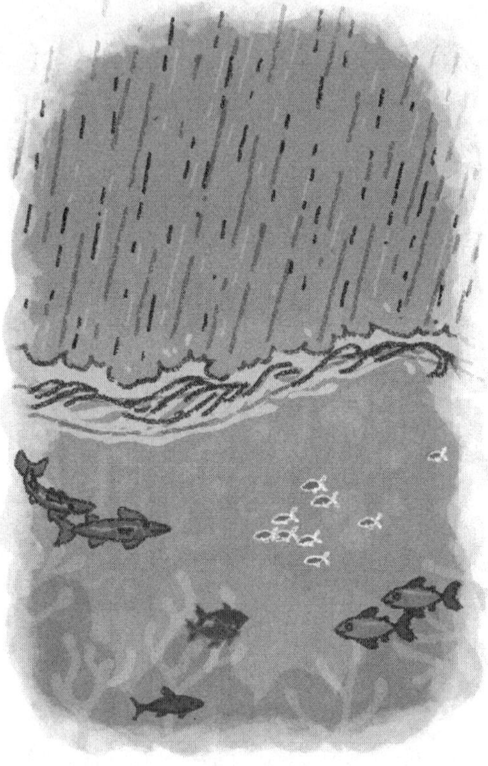

THE DISTANT RAIN

When it rains upon the sea
the raindrops feel like
they're going down to visit
a relative who is a millionaire.

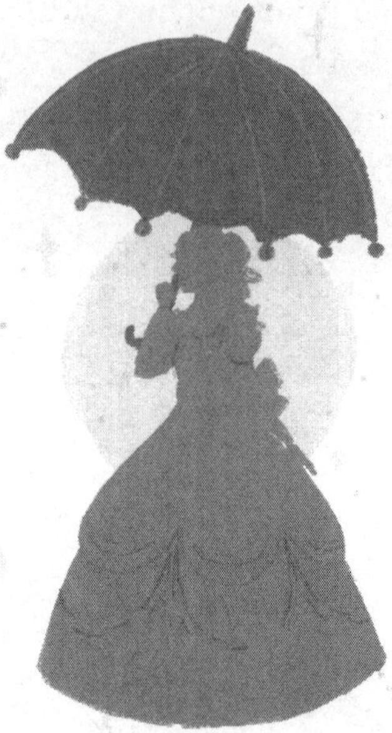

A SPECIAL GIRL

That girl
so small
and so sweet,
crossing
the plaza
under
her red
umbrella,
seemed
like something
out of a storybook.

MYSTERIOUS POEMS

The rain
makes the river break out in spots
and makes the windows
weep.

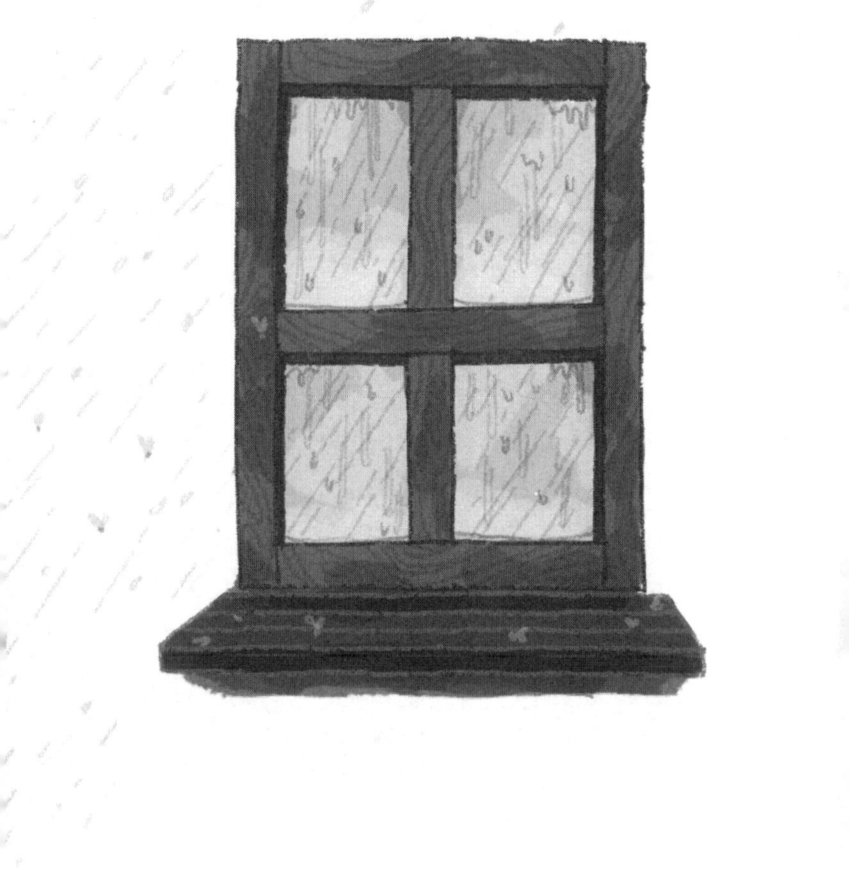

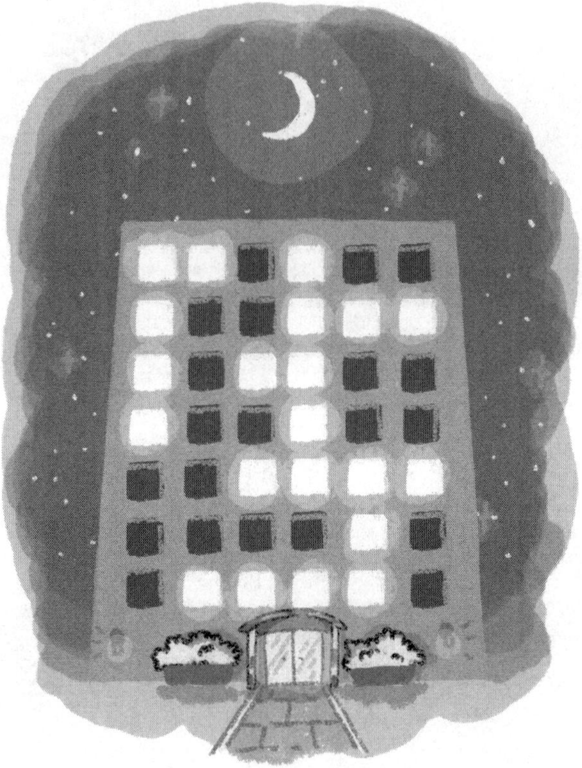

NIGHT

When night begins to fall
and the first apartments turn on their lights,
the buildings that border the plaza
look like gigantic crossword puzzles.

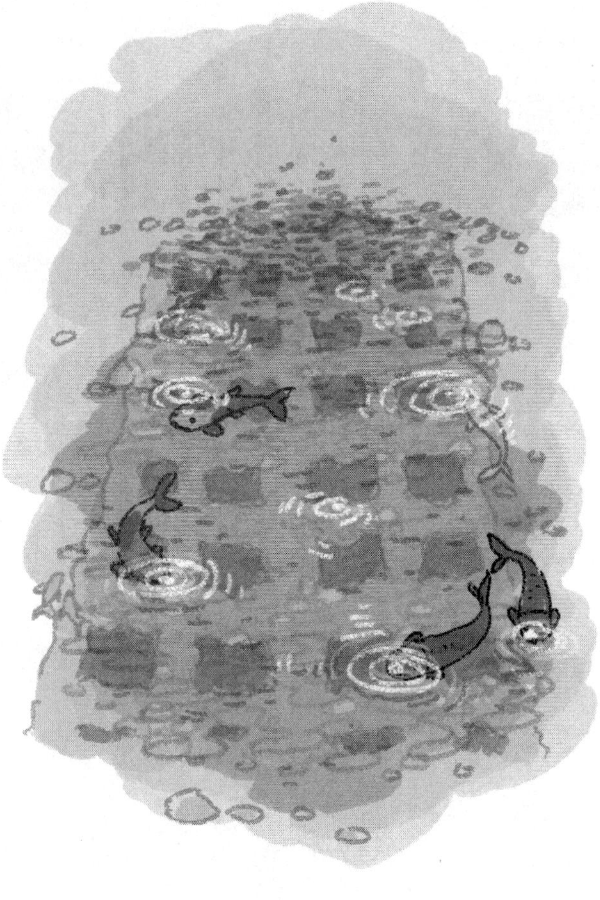

THE HOTEL

The hotel
reflected
in the river,

the fish
crossing
through the hallways.

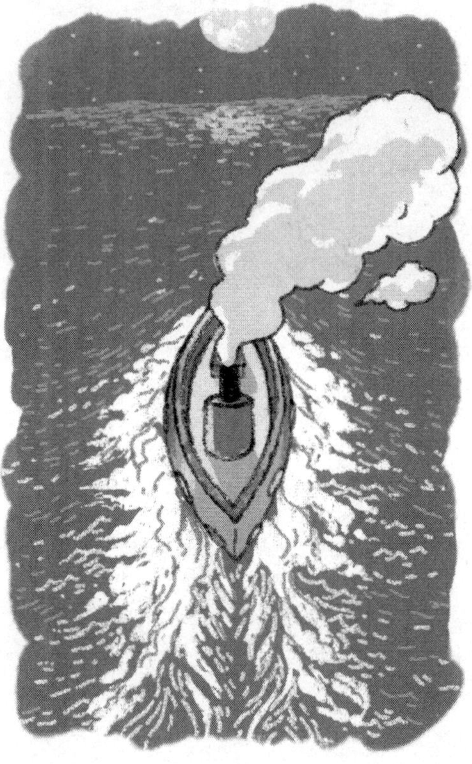

In Some Places

The ship
cuts
the sea.

The sea
bleeds
white foam.

Complicit,
the moon
watches.

DAWNING

That cat –
black,
large,
slow –
walking towards
the wall

turned
the corner

and took
the night
with it.

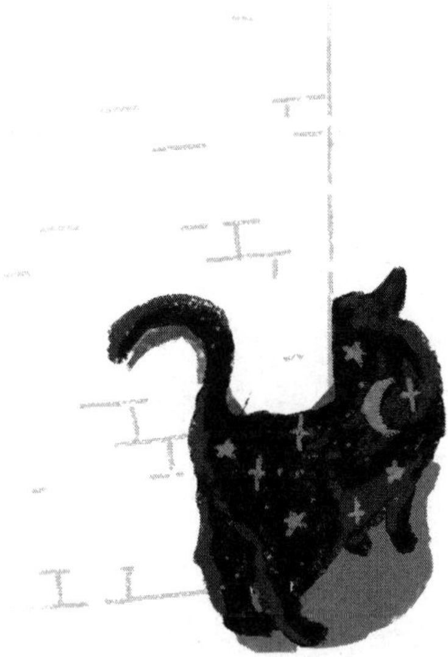

BONUS BITS

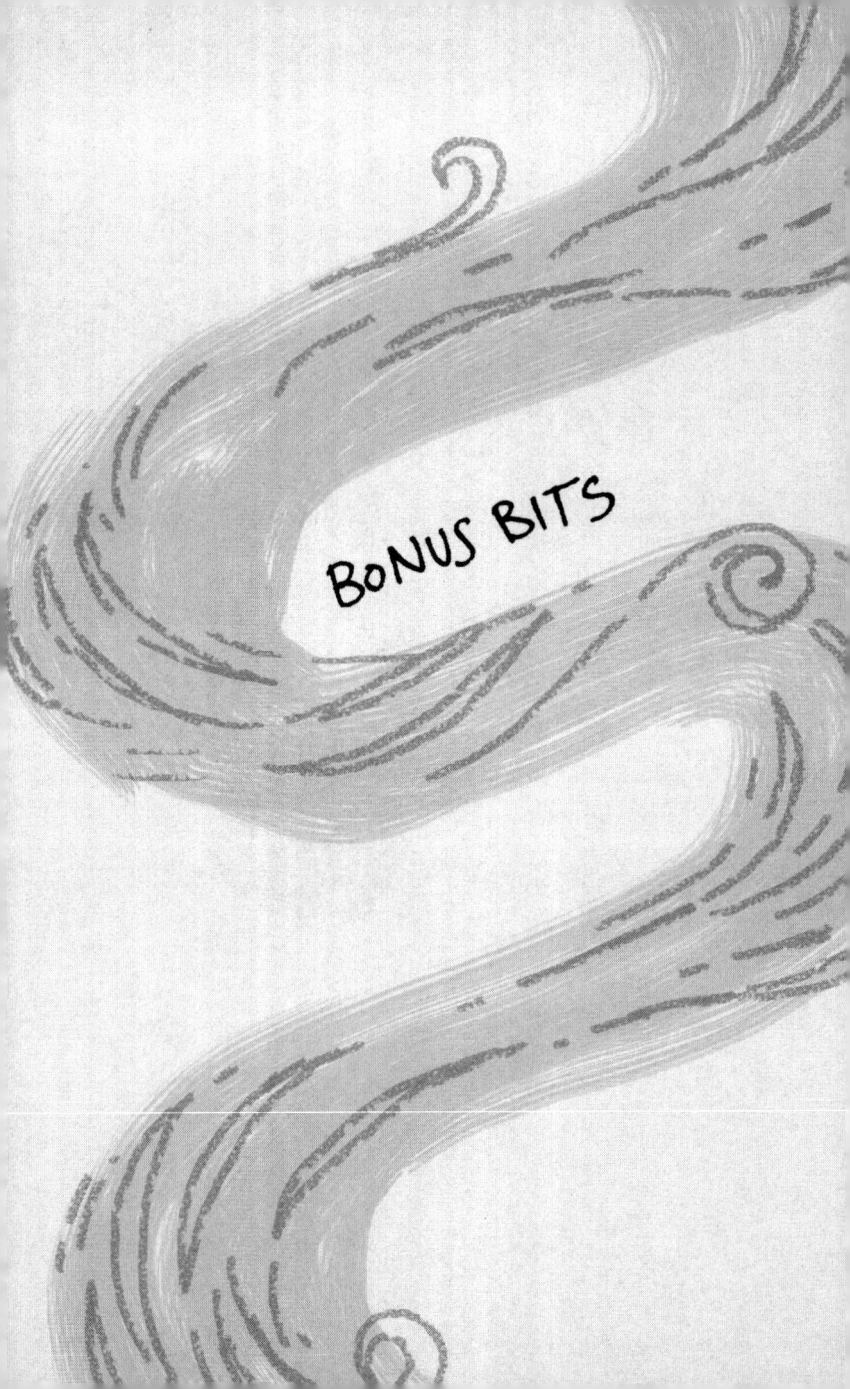

WRITE YOUR OWN POEM

Now it's time to write your own poems – you could illustrate them too!

Here are some ideas to help get you started.

Has a book ever made you feel transported into another world? Pick one of your favourite books and imagine that you have suddenly been dropped inside the action. Now write a poem about it!

You could mention what you first see (and smell) around you, how you feel when you realise where you are, and what you might do after that.

In 'Plastic bag' on page 6, the poet imagines what an everyday object might worry about and wish for. Look around you and pick another ordinary object (a chair? a piece of paper? a shoe?) and write a poem about its hopes and fears.

What's the best thing a chair could wish for? What would be the worst thing that could happen to it?

Next time you take a walk (maybe on your way to school), keep an eye out for something you could write a snapshot poem about, like 'This morning, in the park' on page 16.

It doesn't have to be unusual – it could be something you see every day. Imagine you're taking a photo of it, but with a poem instead of a camera. Make this a very visual poem, with lots of details so the reader can imagine it exactly like it was.

Let's write a train poem! On page 27, the train goes through lots of tunnels, which means the scenery will be different every time the train is out of a tunnel.

Pick three different places you know well and imagine you're on a train going past each of these places. Write a verse for each place, describing what you see out of the window.

Take a look out of the window. Can you see any pairs of things? These could be living things, like a pair of birds or a pair of people, or inanimate objects, like a pair of bicycles. What might they have to talk about?

Imagine a conversation between them and write a poem about it. You could alternate verses between the two, or give each alternate lines.

On page 43, some birds are solving a mystery, but we don't find out what the mystery actually is. Write a poem about what the canary did – it could be anything! What would birds think was a crime? And why did the canary do it? You could write this poem from the point of view of the canary, or from the point of view of the raven, who has been observing the canary.

Next time it rains and you're outside, have a peer in a puddle. What does the world look like from the puddle? What can you see? What looks familiar, and what is distorted? Write a poem about this puddle world, imagining you are a tour guide showing a group of visitors around. What will you point out to them?

INTERVIEW WITH THE TRANSLATOR

The poems in this book were originally written in Spanish, by the poet Karmelo C. Iribarren (you can find out more about him on page 69).

These poems were translated into English by Lawrence Schimel, and we thought you might like to find out a little bit about him...

Hello, Lawrence! First things first: how many languages can you speak?

The only two languages I speak fluently are English and Spanish. Those are the two languages I can create in, and they are the ones I translate between most actively.

When I was in high school I studied the Classics – both Latin and Homeric Greek – which gave me a solid foundation for understanding many other Romance languages (at least reading) not to mention understanding the roots of many words in English.

At university I took a class in Old Norse because I've always loved reading the stories of the Icelandic sagas. But those are what are often called 'dead languages', because no one speaks them any longer in daily use, and I don't claim to speak them either, although I enjoyed studying them.

But I love languages in general, and learning words, concepts, ideas that don't exist in the languages I speak. I feel like I learn to think in a different way, as if these new words help expand not just my vocabulary but my brain.

When I travel I always try to learn some words of the languages of the people I will meet: both so I can be polite and also out of self-preservation: I have many food allergies, so I need to know how to say all the ingredients that will make me sick!

How did you learn Spanish?

I grew up speaking Spanish at home. My mother had studied Spanish literature in Spain and worked as a court interpreter and Spanish speaker.

This was both good and bad: when I started to study Spanish at school, I was put forward a year because I had a decent accent and fluency, but as a result I never had the formal training in grammar. I especially get my verb tenses all mixed up, even to this day.

My favorite Spanish word is 'escampar', which is a verb that describes the moment when the sky clears after it rains and the clouds go away. I had never stopped to recognise that moment, even though I had watched it happen before, until I learned the word for it.

What's the best part about being a translator?

Getting to help bring a book I love to readers who couldn't otherwise be able to read it in the original language.

I also find it lots of fun: it is creative and intellectually stimulating, but it doesn't drain me the way my own writing often does. To me its more like doing a crossword or a Sudoku puzzle; figuring out how make all the many different elements all fit, and that sense of satisfaction when you manage to do so.

What are some of the challenges of translation?

I always try and recreate the same reading experience when I translate, especially in poetry. So if a poem rhymes in the original, or has a lot of wordplay, I try and make sure that those elements are also present in the translation – even if not always in the same place.

Sometimes the words in the translation will lose the alliteration of the original, but in that case I will try and add a similar string of alliteration in another line.

Some concepts are also very culturally specific, so in the translation (especially in fiction) I may need to add an extra few words to explain or contextualise a word.

For instance, in Spain we have the 'merienda', which is a mid-afternoon snack, around 6pm, whereas in many parts of the English-speaking world, people have already had dinner by that same time! (In Spain, dinner is usually served much later, after 9pm.)

What is your favourite poem in *Poems the wind blew in*?

It's always hard to pick just one favourite, but I especially loved the poems about the wind. They made me see something that can't actually be seen, even though we can see its effects upon the world. These poems make me see the world in a different way now: whenever I see a newspaper or book whose pages are being ruffled quickly by a breeze, I think: that wind is speed-reading!

LEARN SOME SPANISH

Lawrence has picked out some words from the original Spanish poems and added how to say them (in brackets). First, here are some tips on pronunciation:

The **ll** sound is pronounced like a **y**.

The **ñ** is pronounced like **nya**.

A double **rr** sound is pronounced by rolling the **r** sound, like a purr.

Both **g** and **j** can sound the same in Spanish, like an **h** sound in English.

The **g** is pronounced soft if it is followed by an **e** or **i** – it is more like an **h** sound in English. But when followed by an **a** or **o** or **u** it is pronounced hard, like in the words **go** or **garden**.

The **h** in Spanish is usually silent.

cat .... **gato** (GAH-to)

wind .... **viento** (vee-EN-to)

rain .... **lluvia** (YU-vee-uh)

tree .... **árbol** (AR-bowl)

book .... **libro** (LEE-bro)

world .... **mundo** (MOON-do)

summer .... **verano** (ver-AN-o)

winter .... **invierno** (in-vee-ER-no)

sky .... **cielo** (see-EL-o)

night .... **noche** (no-chay)

street .... **calle** (cay-ye)

cloud .... **nube** (new-bay)

love .... **amor** (ah-MORE)

clock .... **reloj** (re-LOH)

WHO MADE THIS BOOK?

ABOUT THE POET

Karmelo C. Iribarren (San Sebastián, 1959) is a bestselling poet who has published twelve collections of poetry, as well as various volumes of his selected or complete poems.

In prose, he has published *Diario de K*, which alternates aphorisms, prose poetry and picturesque observations about his city.

This is his first (and so far only) collection of poems for younger readers.

ABOUT THE TRANSLATOR

Lawrence Schimel is a bilingual author and literary translator working in and between English and Spanish. He has published over 100 books as author or anthologist, including poetry pamphlet *Fairy Tales for Writers* (A Midsummer Night's Press), *Will You Read My Book With Me?* (Epigram), *Let's Go See Papá!* (Groundwood), and others. His many awards include a Golden Kite from the Society of Children's Book Writers and Illustrators, a White Raven from the International Youth Library, IBBY Outstanding Books for Youth with Disabilities (twice), and other honours.

He is also a prolific literary translator. Recent translations include the middle grade novel *The Wild Book* by Juan Villoro (Hope Road), picture books *The Band* and *Under the Water*, both written and illustrated by Carles Porta (Flying Eye), and adult poetry collections *We Were Not There* by Jordi Doce and *Bomarzo* by Elsa Cross (both Shearsman). He has lived in Madrid, Spain for the past 20 years.

ABOUT THE ILLUSTRATOR

Riya Chowdhury is an illustrator based in the West Midlands who likes to create fun works of art by trying new methods. She likes to use a lot of colours but also likes to work in black and white.

For more of her work visit her website:
www.ri-ya.co.uk

ABOUT THE EMMA PRESS

The Emma Press is an independent publishing house based in the Jewellery Quarter, Birmingham, UK. It was founded in 2012 by Emma Dai'an Wright. We specialise in poetry, short fiction and children's books.

The Emma Press won the Michael Marks Award for Poetry Pamphlet Publishers in 2016 and Emma Press books have won the Poetry Book Society Pamphlet Choice Award, the Saboteur Award for Best Collaborative Work, and CLiPPA, the CLPE award for children's poetry books.

We publish themed poetry anthologies, single-author poetry and fiction pamphlets (chapbooks), and books for children. We have a growing list of translations which includes titles from Latvia, Estonia, Indonesia, Spain and the Netherlands.

You can find out more about the Emma Press and buy books directly from us here:

theemmapress.com

This book has been selected to receive financial assistance from English PEN's Writers in Translation programme supported by Bloomberg and Arts Council England. English PEN exists to promote literature and its understanding, uphold writers' freedoms around the world, campaign against the persecution and imprisonment of writers for stating their views, and promote the friendly co-operation of writers and free exchange of ideas.

Each year, a dedicated committee of professionals selects books that are translated into English from a wide variety of foreign languages. We award grants to UK publishers to help translate, promote, market and champion these titles. Our aim is to celebrate books of outstanding literary quality, which have a clear link to the PEN charter and promote free speech and intercultural understanding.

In 2011, Writers in Translation's outstanding work and contribution to diversity in the UK literary scene was recognised by Arts Council England. English PEN was awarded a threefold increase in funding to develop its support for world writing in translation.

www.englishpen.org

ENGLISH PEN

FREEDOM TO **WRITE**
FREEDOM TO **READ**

ALSO FROM THE EMMA PRESS

SUPER GUPPY

Poems by Edward van de Vendel, illustrated by Fleur van de Weel and translated from Dutch by David Colmer

Have you ever had a pet? Or have you ever stopped to look at all of the small things in your home that make up your life? From wet socks to being tucked into bed at night, and strongly featuring one inspiring guppy fish with real staying power – *Super Guppy* stays close to home, but it's a home full of fun, jokes, and surprising adventure.

£12.00
Paperback ISBN 978-1-910139-65-3
Poems aimed at children aged 8+

ALSO FROM THE EMMA PRESS

EVERYONE'S THE SMARTEST

Poems by Contra, illustrated by Ulla Saar
Translated from Estonian by Charlotte Geater,
Kätlin Kaldmaa and Richard O'Brien

Everyone's the Smartest is a collection of poems which tell strange new stories in familiar settings. From clever ducks who fly far away while children are stuck in school, to bathroom taps that are just one mistake away from turning the school into a great lake, this collection reminds its readers that there is wonder everywhere.

£12.00
Paperback ISBN 978-1-910139-99-8
Poems aimed at children aged 8+

ALSO FROM THE EMMA PRESS

THE BOOK OF CLOUDS

Poems by Juris Kronbergs, illustrated by Anete Melece and translated from Latvian by Mara Rozitis and Richard O'Brien.

If you look up on a cloudy day, you'll see a whole new surprising world above you – the world of clouds! A mix of dreamy fantasy and scientific fact, this is the perfect gift for any child with their head stuck in the clouds – and for anyone who has ever wondered what's up there in the skies above.

£12.00
Hardback ISBN 978-1-910139-14-1
Poems aimed at children aged 8+